CLIMBING IN THE DARK

NICK WARBURTON

Illustrated by Martin Cottam

D1137017

OXFORD
UNIVERSITY PRESS

OXFORD
UNIVERSITY PRESS

Great Clarendon Street, Oxford OX2 6DP

Oxford University Press is a department of the University of Oxford.
It furthers the University's objective of excellence in research, scholarship,
and education by publishing worldwide in

Oxford   New York

Auckland   Cape Town   Dar es Salaam   Hong Kong   Karachi
Kuala Lumpur   Madrid   Melbourne   Mexico City   Nairobi
New Delhi   Shanghai   Taipei   Toronto

With offices in

Argentina   Austria   Brazil   Chile   Czech Republic   France   Greece
Guatemala   Hungary   Italy   Japan   Poland   Portugal   Singapore
South Korea   Switzerland   Thailand   Turkey   Ukraine   Vietnam

Oxford is a registered trade mark of Oxford University Press
in the UK and in certain other countries

British Library Cataloguing in Publication Data
Data available

ISBN: 978-0-19-918407-1

20 19 18

Available in packs
Stage 14 Pack of 6:
ISBN: 978-0-19-918406-4
Stage 14 Class Pack:
ISBN: 978-0-19-918413-2
Guided Reading Cards also available:
ISBN: 978-0-19-918415-6

Cover artwork by Martin Cottam
Photograph Nick Warburton © Eaden Lilley Photography

Printed in Malaysia by
MunSang Printers Sdn Bhd

Paper used in the production of this book is a natural, recyclable product
made from wood grown in sustainable forests. The manufacturing process
conforms to the environmental regulations of the country of origin.

CHAPTER 1

Tess

When I was twelve, my mother found me a job as housemaid to a gentleman's family. I remember looking up at Dr Gooch's front door on my first day. It was a black door, with a brass knocker shaped like a snake coiled round a stick. The snake frightened me, and I felt like running away, but I knew I had to knock. When I did, the sound boomed through the house.

I seemed to be there ages before the door swung open and a lady with a red round face appeared.

'Please, ma'am,' I said, 'I'm Tess ...'

'Ah, the new housemaid. But you've come to the wrong door, girl. Only proper visitors come to this door. The servants come in by the door round the back.'

'I'm sorry, ma'am, I didn't know.'

'And don't call me ma'am. I'm a housekeeper, not a lady. You must call me Mrs Hutton.'

She pulled me into the hall and shut the door. And there I was, in that grand house, with the outside world shut off.

'You'll sleep in the attic,' Mrs Hutton told me. 'But first you must come down to the kitchen and have some milk. Then I can tell you all you need to know.'

She led the way across the marble
hall. The floor was patterned with black
and white squares, and our feet clicked
on the marble and made echoes.

A tall man with side whiskers was
hurrying down a staircase towards us.
Mrs Hutton curtsied and stood quietly
with her hands folded in front of her. I
thought it best to do the same. The
man wore a dark coat, very smart, with
tails, and a stiff white collar. He looked
most severe.

'See that the coach comes to the door at three this afternoon, Mary,' he said. 'We're taking tea with the Athertons.'

He was about to go away, but he noticed me and stopped.

'And who is this?'

I bowed my head and said nothing.

'This is Tess, Dr Gooch. The new housemaid.'

'Tess,' he said. 'Well, if you are a good girl I'm sure you will be happy here.'

But he frowned as he said it and I couldn't imagine ever being happy in his house.

'Now then,' said Mrs Hutton when he'd gone, 'let's get down to the kitchen before anything else crops up.'

But something else cropped up straight away. There was a knock at the front door.

'My stars, it's the mistress, back from her walk,' said Mrs Hutton.

There on the step was a lady in a cloak of the most beautiful material. Behind her stood a girl of about my age, and bouncing around at their feet was a little dog all done up in ribbons and bows.

'Stand still, Belle!' said the lady, coming into the hall and handing her cloak to Mrs Hutton.

She didn't seem to notice I was there.

'This silly creature has been rolling in all the puddles, Mary. Look at the mud on her ribbons.'

'She was only enjoying herself, Mama,' said the girl. 'I can soon clean her.'

'No, Harriet, you cannot. Young ladies don't scrub dirty little dogs like this.'

Mrs Gooch bent down and scooped up the wriggling Belle. Then, holding the little thing at arms' length, she thrust her at me. I was so startled to be noticed I nearly dropped her.

'Here,' said Mrs Gooch. 'Take her away.'

Harriet glanced at me and sighed.
'And don't sigh like that, Harriet.
Young ladies never make such ugly
sounds.'

Then she swept across the hall to the staircase. She went upstairs – so smoothly and so gracefully – calling behind her, 'That silly creature has quite tired me out. I must take a nap.'

Harriet watched her and sighed again.

'Oh, Mary,' she said, 'I'm never allowed to do anything. I have to be so pretty and polite all the time. I hate it.'

Then she looked straight at me.

'Oh,' she said. 'You're new. What's your name?'

'Tess, miss,' I stammered.

'May I help you, Tess? Please?'

'Go on, miss,' said Mrs Hutton before I could answer. 'Up to the nursery, or I'll get it in the neck from your Mama.'

'Nursery!' said Harriet, making for the staircase. 'I hate that too. Perhaps one day something interesting will happen in this house.'

CHAPTER 2

The chimney sweep

Once we were safely in Mrs Hutton's warm kitchen, she seemed to relax. She poured me some milk from a stone jug and plomped herself down at the table.

'You can give Belle a scrub out in the scullery,' she said, nodding at an outer door. 'It'll be your first job.'

As she spoke there came a thump at the door, and I jumped and spilled the milk.

'Oh no,' said Mrs Hutton. 'Not him.'

She got up slowly and fetched a cloth to wipe the milk. The knocking came again.

'Shall I open it?' I asked.

'It's Mr Fry,' she said. 'And he can wait.'

Only when she'd mopped up the milk did she let Mr Fry in. He stood in the doorway with the light behind him, like a great thick shadow.

'What kept you?' he growled, stooping to enter.

'We're busy down here, Mr Fry,' said Mrs Hutton coldly.

His face was smeared with grime so that only his eyes showed, and he had a bundle of canes under his arm. He flung them on the floor and turned to shout back at the door.

'Don't stand out there gawping, you little rat. Fetch in some of them poles.'

At first I thought he was talking to Mrs Hutton, and I was horrified. But it wasn't that.

A little crouching figure now appeared in the doorway. It was even grimier than Mr Fry, but it was frail and bent, like a timid animal.

'You've got a new boy, I see, Mr Fry,' said Mrs Hutton.

'A boy, Mrs Hutton? A rat on two legs more like. And an expensive one, too.'

The boy edged into the kitchen and stooped to put the poles down. Then he started to cough. He stayed bent, holding his knees, and his thin back shook.

'Why, he's skinny as railings,' Mrs Hutton began.

'Of course he's skinny. He's got to get up chimneys, hasn't he? If he was plump he'd get stuck.'

So then I knew – Mr Fry was the chimney sweep.

'What he needs is a little water,' Mrs Hutton said with a fierce frown.

'He needs a clout round the ear ...'

'Water, Mr Fry. You take your things through and I'll see to the boy. Go on, Mr Fry. I'll bring him to you in two shakes.'

'Don't you pamper the little brat, that's all,' mumbled Mr Fry, shuffling off with his poles and brushes.

Mrs Hutton glared after him. Then she took the boy by the elbow and sat him down at the table where his coughing started again.

'You ought to be home in bed, my chicken,' she told him.

'I ain't got no bed. I got a bit of straw on the floor.'

'What's your name, boy?'

'Will.'

'Will what?'

'Just Will. I don't know no other name. My father sold me to Mr Fry, to go up chimbleys.'

'Sold you?' I said. 'Your own father?'

'Yes. 'E took me to Fry's 'ouse one day and then went 'ome without me. I found meself in this cellar full of brushes and things. Then I knowed. I was sold, to go up chimbleys.'

'But that's terrible.'

'That's fathers for you, miss. They're all the same.'

'What ever must it be like, climbing about in chimneys?' said Mrs Hutton with a glance at me.

'It's 'orrible, miss. The bricks stay so 'ot it 'urts, and the chimbley's dark and it twists about so you don't know where you are. And Mr Fry, 'e puts vinegar on me elbows and knees and stands me before the fire till I'm nearly roasted up.'

'But why does he do that?' I asked.

'To 'arden the skin, miss. So I can grip on the chimbleys.'

Mrs Hutton was quiet for a while. Then she said, 'Well, Will, there's some milk, and there's a spoon, and there's a pot of honey. You help yourself to that.'

As Will struggled to put the spoon in the pot, she turned her back on him and wiped her face with her apron. He tucked into the milk and honey, his elbows flapping and his face becoming sticky as well as grimy.

'I 'ave to go,' he said at last, wiping his hands on his ragged trousers. 'He'll smack me about if I don't get back to him.'

CHAPTER 3

Will loses his way

I laid out my things in the little attic room and looked at them. I didn't have very much – a prayer book, my mother's old needle-case and a rag doll – but the sight of them made me think about poor Will who had nothing at all.

There was a black dress and a starched white apron spread out on the bed for me to wear. They were too big for me, but I put them on and they made me feel very grand.

I went to the top of the attic stairs and tried to remember the way back to the kitchen. Then I heard a terrible bellowing shout somewhere below me. I couldn't make out the words but I could tell they were angry, and I feared that someone was calling for me. I clattered down the attic steps and ran into Mr Fry. He was pacing up and down, punching one hand with the other.

'He's gone!' he shouted at me. 'The skinny rat's gone!'

Mrs Hutton, red in the face and holding her skirts in both hands, was running up the main staircase.

'Mr Fry!' she said. 'Whatever is all this racket?'

'That ratbag of a boy's gone up the chimney but he ain't come down.'

'Oh, my stars. The poor mite!'

'Poor? I'll have his bones for broth when I get hold of him.'

Mrs Hutton took a deep breath and clapped her hands, as if that would be enough to calm him down.

'Don't clap at me, missus. I ain't a bird.'

'Then stop flapping. He hasn't done it on purpose, has he?'

He scowled and was about to answer back when there was another shout, a high-pitched scream which came from the other end of the corridor.

'Lawks!' said Mrs Hutton. 'It's Miss Harriet. Come along, Tess. We must see what's up.'

She bustled down the corridor, leaving me to follow.

'What about the missing rat?' Mr Fry called after her.

'He's just taking a rest, poor thing. He'll turn up.'

'But …'

'Don't make a fuss, Mr Fry,' said Mrs Hutton, turning so sharply to shout at him that I almost bumped into her. 'You know where he went. Why don't you stick your head up the chimney and look for him!'

And she hurried away before he could answer. She wheeled round a corner, tilting like a cart stacked with hay. By this time the shouting was much fainter, as if Harriet had run out of breath.

We came to her door and Mrs Hutton
flung it open.

I saw a pretty room with lace curtains
at the window, two little padded chairs,
and a huge, shiny rocking-horse in the
middle of the floor. There was no sign
of Miss Harriet but we heard her
trembling voice.

'Help me, Mary. Please.'

She was crouched in a corner, her
hands over her ears.

'There, there, Miss Harriet,' said
Mrs Hutton. 'You're quite safe ...'

'There's a creature in here.
A monster ...'

She pointed with a shaking finger and we saw a black heap on the floor behind the rocking-horse. I knew at once what it was, but I couldn't understand how it came to be there.

'I think it's Will,' I said.

'Oo-er, so it is,' said Mrs Hutton.

'Please, get rid of it,' said Harriet. 'It's left paw prints on the rugs and ...' – she gulped for air and screamed again – 'it's *moving!'*

Mrs Hutton ran to Harriet and folded her in her arms.

'He won't harm you, miss. It's only Will.'

'Will?'

'The chimney sweep's boy. He must've fallen down the chimney and knocked himself out.'

'I don't care what it is, Mary. Just get rid of it.'

'He's not an it; he's a boy.'

Will sat up and rubbed his head. He was so covered in soot that he looked like a big black bird, and there were powdery splashes on the floor around him.

'Where am I?' he moaned. 'What's going on?'

'You're in the nursery, boy,' Mrs Hutton told him. 'You've come down the wrong chimney.'

He blinked and two white eyes
appeared in his face. Harriet broke free
of Mrs Hutton and dashed to a cord
hanging by the door.

She's going to pull the bell, I thought.
She's going to call the whole house in
here and get poor Will taken away.

Mrs Hutton caught her by the wrist.

'Now you just calm yourself, miss,'
she said. 'The little lad's hurt himself
and we can't go giving him back to old
Fry just yet ...'

'But why not?'

'Because he'll beat him, that's why
not,' said Mrs Hutton crossly.

I was amazed that she spoke to her like that. But Harriet did as she was told. She calmed down and pressed herself against the wall, as far from Will as she could get. Mrs Hutton went over to the boy and knelt beside him. She sat him up, gently stroking his face and hair.

'Can't you see?' she said to Harriet. 'He's had a fright.'

Will was shaking, and he'd started to cough again. Mrs Hutton rubbed his back and spoke to him in a soft, kindly voice. Harriet edged away from the wall and came to stand behind Mrs Hutton. She could see now that there was no monster in her room, only a poor frightened boy.

'But what's the matter with him?' she said.

So Mrs Hutton told her. She told her everything Will had told us, and Harriet listened like a child hearing fairy tales.

'So we can't hand him over just yet, can we?' finished Mrs Hutton.

'No, Mary. We certainly can't.'

Just then there were heavy footsteps in the corridor, and I ran over to the door and peeped out.

'It's Mr Fry,' I said. 'And Dr Gooch. They're trying all the doors!'

'Then we must hide the boy,' said Harriet. She gave a quick, determined look around the room.

'And we must clear up this mess. Put him in the toy cupboard, Mary. And Tess, help me to tidy up!'

'Yes, miss. Right away, miss.'

We worked side by side, sweeping and tidying like three servants instead of two, to keep poor Will safe.

When we had finished we stood quite still and listened. Doors slammed. The voices came nearer. They were both very angry by now.

'Your Papa's awfully angry, Miss Harriet,' Mrs Hutton said softly. 'Perhaps we ought to let them know he's here, and make up some excuse for the lad.'

'No,' said Harriet.'We shan't hand him over at all. We'll set him free!'

Mrs Hutton's mouth was wide with surprise, but before she could say another word, the nursery door burst open.

CHAPTER 4

Harriet

'He must be here,' Fry said. 'We've looked every other blooming place.'

'Please, sir. Control your language in front of my daughter.'

Harriet looked at me and grinned.

'Beg pardon for barging in, missie,' said Fry, 'but have you seen a rat-faced scrawny bean-pole pass through?'

'A what?'

'Mr Fry's boy has gone missing,' said Dr Gooch. 'Has he been in here?'

'Of course not, Papa.'

'That's odd, then,' said Fry with a sly look. 'The boy goes missing, and there's screams in this room ...'

'Mr Fry,' said Dr Gooch sternly, 'if my daughter says she has not seen him, you may take her word for it. I suggest we go downstairs and look there.'

And he frowned so severely that Fry began to back out of the room.

Then Will coughed.

Both men stopped in the doorway and looked at each other. Mrs Hutton began to choke and splutter, as if it had been her, but it was no good. There was another cough and Fry strode back into the nursery, flung open the cupboard, and Will tumbled out.

'Got you, you scheming bag of bones!' snarled Fry, grabbing Will by the shoulder.

Dr Gooch frowned at Harriet and beneath his dark eyebrows his eyes were burning with anger.

'You must have known he was there, Harriet,' he said in a low voice.

'She didn't, mister,' coughed Will. 'I 'id meself and she didn't know nothing about it ...'

'Be quiet, child!' shouted Dr Gooch, so loud and sudden that it made me jump. 'Take him out, Fry. Harriet, I shall speak to you about this later.'

Fry dragged Will to his feet, the door
banged shut and the room fell silent.
The three of us looked hopelessly at
each other.

'We've made it worse for the lad
now,' said Mrs Hutton at last. 'And Dr
Gooch could turn me out for this.'

'He can't!'

'You know he can, Miss Harriet, and
you know what it'll mean if he does.
It'll be the end of me.'

She took her apron in both hands
and buried her face in it.

'If you are turned out, Mary, I shall run away,' Harriet said firmly. 'But we must find that boy first. I won't have him beaten.'

She crossed to the window and stared out, thinking. 'If only we knew where Fry lives,' she said to herself.

I looked quickly at Mrs Hutton. Her plump face was lined with worry. She had a good job – a roof over her head and respect – and she was scared of losing it. I couldn't bear to think of this kind motherly lady turned out on to the streets. The shame of it … and no one to give her milk and honey …

Suddenly Harriet gave a little cry and spun round to us with her eyes shining.

'Do you hear that?' she said. 'It's Fry's cart rolling down the street. With his name and address painted on the side. Now we know where he lives!'

'Where is it, miss?' I asked.

'A place called Cobble Yard. Do you know where that is, Mary?'

Mrs Hutton sniffed and wiped her eyes with her apron.

'Yes, miss,' she said quietly. 'It's down by the river, near the big bridge.'

'Then you can go there,' cried Harriet. 'You can go there and find poor Will.'

She sounded so pleased and excited. She hardly noticed that Mrs Hutton was upset. It wasn't really her fault. She didn't know what it was like to be a servant. She was only thinking of how she could help Will.

'Yes, miss. Of course, miss,' sighed Mrs Hutton.

'I know Cobble Yard, Miss Harriet,' I said quickly. 'Will you let me go? Please, miss. I can be ever so quick and nimble.'

'No, Tess,' Mrs Hutton said quickly. 'This is your first day and ...'

'But Mrs Hutton, I know the place. And I'm young and I can nip about so no one knows I'm there.'

'That's right, Tess,' said Miss Harriet, taking hold of my hands. 'You must go. Thank you, thank you.'

So that was decided. I took a deep breath and sighed. I knew what I was doing – going instead of Mrs Hutton, going to help poor Will. And if Dr Gooch found out, I'd be the one to lose my job. I didn't know if my mother would understand that.

I closed my eyes and seemed to hear her voice.

'Why, Tess? Why did you throw it all away? You've been disgraced. You'll never get another chance now. Oh, what's to become of us? What's to become of us?'

But there was no time to think about all that now. Harriet was pacing up and down and talking fast.

'Our carriage goes right by the river,' she said, 'so we can take you.'

'No, no, Miss Harriet,' said Mrs Hutton. 'That'll never do. How can poor Tess go with you in the carriage? What would your Papa say?'

'Not *in* the carriage, Mary. At the back. Under the flap where we put the cases.' Harriet said to me, 'Just find out where Will is and tell us what you see. That will be enough to start with.'

Mrs Hutton took me down to the servants' door at the back of the house, and sneaked me outside. We waited by an iron gate and peered into the street. There was a neat black carriage waiting by Dr Gooch's front door. A coachman stood by two chestnut horses and stroked their necks.

'There's a canvas sheet at the back of the carriage,' hissed Mrs Hutton. 'Nip under that, as quick as you can.'

I was about to dart away when she took hold of my hand and squeezed it.

'You are a brave girl, Tess,' she said. 'Thank you.'

I just smiled at her.

'If things do go wrong,' she whispered, 'I'll do what I can for you. I won't let you go hungry. Go now. And good luck!'

Then I ran, as hard as I could, to the back of the carriage. I saw the canvas sheet, scrabbled under it and I found myself on a dusty wooden platform. A little light filtered through the canvas, green and shadowy, and there was a damp, musty smell.

I could hear nothing but the thumping of my own heart and the horses stamping now and again.

There I stayed, perfectly still and curled up. My mind was spinning with all that had happened – with fear of being discovered; and with wondering what on earth I'd do if I did find Will. Then I heard the front door bang and felt the carriage rock as people climbed in. The wheels began to grind against the cobbles and it was too late to wonder any more. We were moving.

In no time at all I was jolted from side to side like a cabbage in a wheelbarrow. I thought I was going to be knocked senseless at any moment, but I clung on and, after what seemed ages, we rolled to a halt.

I got to my knees and tried to peer out, but the shadow of an arm passed over the canvas sheet. Light flooded in, hurting my eyes. Someone leant over me.

CHAPTER 5

Discovery!

'Tess, it's me. Harriet.'

I blinked and Harriet's face appeared. Her eyes were wide and she was smiling.

'Fry's place is just over the road,' she said in a rush. 'There. Can you see?'

I followed her pointing finger.

'But your father,' I said. 'Won't he …'

'He thinks I'm looking for my handkerchief. I dropped it out of the window so we had to stop. Wasn't that clever? Jump out, Tess, before they come looking.'

She took my arm and helped me out. As my feet touched the ground the carriage rocked, once, then again. Harriet looked nervously over her shoulder.

'Papa's coming,' she said, giving me a little push. 'Run, Tess.'

My legs tingled and shook, but I staggered away and darted through a group of children playing with a hoop. They shouted at me but I took no notice. When I turned back, Harriet was still by the carriage, her hands behind her back and her head bowed. Dr Gooch was standing over her.

'What's the matter, child?' I heard him shout. 'Where is your handkerchief?'

Harriet mumbled something I couldn't hear. I turned away and left her to her father's anger.

I was in a narrow lane which sloped
steeply down to the right. It was
hemmed in on both sides by tall
buildings with clammy grey walls. In
front of me were railings and some
steps leading down to a small dark yard.
On the railings was a peeling sign. I
couldn't make out many words but one
was clear enough: FRY.

He was down there, somewhere
beyond that dark, damp yard, and I
would have to go and see.

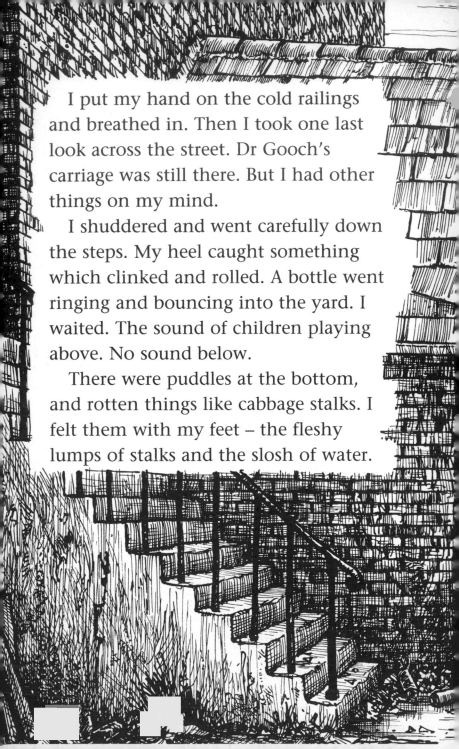

I put my hand on the cold railings and breathed in. Then I took one last look across the street. Dr Gooch's carriage was still there. But I had other things on my mind.

I shuddered and went carefully down the steps. My heel caught something which clinked and rolled. A bottle went ringing and bouncing into the yard. I waited. The sound of children playing above. No sound below.

There were puddles at the bottom, and rotten things like cabbage stalks. I felt them with my feet – the fleshy lumps of stalks and the slosh of water.

I made out a door and touched it with the tips of my fingers. It swung open a little and yellow light spilled into the yard.

I put my head round the door. A dingy room, with a table in the middle. More bottles on the table. A candle in one of them. It flickered in the draught from the door.

Then I saw Fry.

He was slumped in an old armchair, his head lolling on one side. He was asleep.

On the wall above his head were two or three hooks. A hat on one, a large ring with keys on another. There was no sign of Will but I saw another door in the corner of the room.

That's it, I thought. That's where he is. If I could only get hold of those keys ...

Keeping my eyes on the sleeping Fry, I moved step by step across the room. The hardest part was getting hold of the keys because I had to stand close to his chair to reach them; close enough to touch him. I wanted to snatch them and run, but I knew I couldn't do that. The safest way was to go slowly.

I carried the keys – gently, gently – to the door. I tried one, then another. The lock turned with a faint click and the door opened.

Then I heard someone rustling in
straw, scuttling away to a far corner.

'Don't 'it me again, mister ...'

His voice was shrill and scared.
Behind me Fry spluttered and dragged
himself out of his chair. I darted blindly
into the gloom, holding my arms out to
feel my way. I caught a scrap of rag and
grabbed it.

'Let go of me!'

'It's me,' I shouted. 'It's Tess!'

I pulled him towards the door, but
Fry was already there. He filled the
doorway, a dark shape with thin candle-
light behind him.

'Thief!' he bellowed. 'I'm being
robbed!'

He grabbed at us. Will didn't know
what was happening and struggled in
my grasp. He fell, dragging me over,
and I felt wet straw against my face.
Then Fry blundered in, shouting and
cursing. His knee banged into my back
and he went down like a tree. The
thump as he landed made the floor
shake.

'Get out, Will!' I screamed, crawling towards the door. 'Get out!'

And suddenly we were in the outer room. I reached back for the door and slammed it. I turned the key. The lock clicked and there was a terrible roar from Fry.

'Let me out! Let me out of here!'

I took Will by the hand and ran, bumping into the table and knocking the candle over. It flared for a second and then went out. We reached the yard and clambered up the steps to the fresh air and the street above.

Run! I thought. It doesn't matter where. Just run!

Below us I could hear Fry shouting and hammering at the locked door. I grabbed the railings at the top of the steps. But our way was blocked. We ran straight into a man coming up the lane.

It was a tall man in a black coat. I crashed against him and fell backwards on the pavement. Will grabbed the railings and started to sob. The man stooped over me. I saw a frowning face and heavy eyebrows.

'What do you think you're doing?' said Dr Gooch.

But I was too breathless to answer
him. Too breathless, and too afraid.
Then I saw that Harriet was there, too,
clinging on to his sleeve.

'Oh, Tess,' she said. 'You've got him.'

'This is disgraceful,' said Dr Gooch.
'You have no right to do this ...'

'But I told you, Papa. That man is
cruel ...'

'I know what you told me, Harriet. That's why we came back. But this stupid girl has caused no end of trouble and I shall have to put it right.'

He turned back to me.

'Where is Mr Fry now?'

He followed my glance down the steps to the yard where more muffled shouting and banging drifted up to us.

'What is that noise?'

'It's Mr Fry, sir,' I managed to say. 'I've locked him in.'

'Oh, well done!' said Harriet.

'Quiet, Harriet! She has not done well; she has done very badly.'

He leaned forward so that his face was close to mine, and lowered his voice so that only I could hear.

'I see now. You are to blame for everything. You have led my daughter astray. I should, perhaps, call the police.'

'Please, sir, no,' I whispered.

'You have tried to steal Fry's apprentice away from him. The police will tell you that.'

He stared hard at me for a moment.

'I will let you off this time, girl,' he went on in the same low tone, 'but I cannot have you in my house. Do you understand me? You must collect your things and leave this evening.'

I tried to speak but my lip was trembling and warm tears were running down my cheeks.

'Now take me to Fry,' he said, raising his voice again.

Just then Will let go of the railings and threw himself at my legs.

'Please!' he cried. 'Don't make me go back!'

'Now, boy,' Dr Gooch said to him. 'You know you must.'

He put a hand on Will's shoulder, and Will twisted away. His rag of a shirt was pulled to one side.

'Oh!' said Harriet, and she put her hand to her mouth.

Will's poor white back was criss-crossed with red and brown stripes and beads of crusted blood. Dr Gooch stared at them, his eyes wide with shock and his face suddenly pale. For some moments he said nothing. Then he asked quietly, 'How did you get these marks?'

'My master beat me, sir,' Will sobbed.
'For being so bad. Please, don't make
me go back.'

Dr Gooch looked back at me and I
could see a change come over his face. I
could see shock and puzzlement in his
eyes, and at last, understanding.

'Did you know he was beaten like
this?' he asked, and I nodded.

'Well, then,' he said, 'I think you'd
better show me where this man Fry is.'

CHAPTER 6

The new boy

I didn't lose my job with the Gooches.
In fact, I became very happy in that
house. I found out that Dr Gooch had a
strict and severe manner, but that he
was a good man – a most kind man –
when you got to know him. He could
not stand bad manners, but cruelty
made him angry.

And Harriet became my friend – as far
as a servant and a lady can be friends.

She and I would sit at the kitchen table and tell Mrs Hutton the story of Will's rescue. Mrs Hutton never tired of hearing about it, and she never let us miss out a single detail.

'Oh,' she would say, 'but that is terrible. That man should be sent away to the other side of the world.'

He wasn't, though. There was nothing the law could do about the cruel Mr Fry. But Dr Gooch went to see him from time to time.

'To see that he is behaving himself,' he said.

And Mr Fry was so afraid of the stern doctor that I do think he tried to be more gentle with his apprentices after that.

And Will? Well, shortly after that, another new servant joined the household – a poor thin little boy – whose job it was to clean the shoes. And very happy he was to see how bright and shiny he could make them.

About the author

I was a teacher for ten years and enjoyed, above all, sharing stories with my classes.

I now work in a little office in Cambridge, playing with words and making up stories. I consider myself lucky to be able to do that. My writing takes me to all sorts of interesting places and once included a visit to West Africa.

I have also written for radio and television and this story started life as a short play for radio.